What Kids Say About
Carole Marsh Mysteries . . .

I love the real locations! Reading the book always makes me want to go and visit them all on our next family vacation. My Mom says maybe, but I can't wait!

One day, I want to be a real kid in one of Ms. Marsh's mystery books. I think it would be fun, and I think I am a real character anyway. I filled out the application and sent it in and am keeping my fingers crossed!

History was not my favorite subject until I starting reading Carole Marsh Mysteries. Ms. Marsh really brings history to life. Also, she leaves room for the scary and fun.

I think Christina is so smart and brave. She is lucky to be in the mystery books because she gets to go to a lot of places. I always wonder just how much of the book is true and what is made up. Trying to figure that out is fun!

Grant is cool and funny! He makes me laugh a lot!!

I like that there are boys a̶̶̶̶̶̶̶̶ ages. Some mysteries I ou̶ vorite character to identify

They are scary, but not to̶ lot. There is always food which makes me hungry ̶ ̶ ̶ke I am there.

What Parents and Teachers Say About Carole Marsh Mysteries . . .

I think kids love these books because they have such a wealth of detail. I know I learn a lot reading them! It's an engaging way to look at the history of any place or event. I always say I'm only going to read one chapter to the kids, but that never happens—it's always two or three, at least!
—Librarian

Reading the mystery and going on the field trip—Scavenger Hunt in hand—was the most fun our class ever had! It really brought the place and its history to life. They loved the real kids characters and all the humor. I loved seeing them learn that reading is an experience to enjoy! —4th grade teacher

Carole Marsh is really on to something with these unique mysteries. They are so clever; kids want to read them all. The Teacher's Guides are chock full of activities, recipes, and additional fascinating information. My kids thought I was an expert on the subject—and with this tool, I felt like it!
—3rd grade teacher

My students loved writing their own mystery book!
Ms. Marsh's reproducible guidelines are a real jewel. They learned about copyright and ended up with their own book they were so proud of!
—Reading/Writing Teacher

"The kids seem very realistic—my children seemed to relate to the characters. Also, it is educational by expanding their knowledge about the famous places in the books."

"They are what children like: mysteries and adventures with children they can relate to."

"Encourages reading for pleasure."

"This series is great. It can be used for reluctant readers, and as a history supplement."

MASTERS OF DISASTERS™

THE HORRENDOUS HURRICANE MYSTERY

By
Carole Marsh

Published by Gallopade International/Carole Marsh Books. Printed in the
United States of America.

Managing Editor: Sherry Moss
Senior Editor: Janice Baker
Assistant Editor: Fran Kramer
Cover Design & Illustrations: John Kovaleski (www.kovaleski.com)
Content Design: Darryl Lilly, Outreach Graphics

Gallopade International is introducing SAT words that kids need to know
in each new book that we publish. The SAT words are bold in the story.
Look for this special logo beside each word in the glossary. Happy Learning!

Gallopade is proud to be a member and supporter of these educational
organizations and associations:

American Booksellers Association

American Library Association

International Reading Association

National Association for Gifted Children

The National School Supply and Equipment Association

The National Council for the Social Studies

Museum Store Association

Association of Partners for Public Lands

A Note From the Author

When I was a kid, I thought a hurricane was called a "hurry cane," because it came in such a hurry! Later, I learned that a hurricane can sure take its own sweet time to come ashore—but LOOK OUT when it does!

During my first hurricane adventure, my kids and I were so excited. We were inland from the coast (but on the water), so we weren't really scared—a big mistake. It was like a party with everyone getting ready by putting up their garbage cans and porch furniture, buying extra food and supplies, and helping older neighbors get prepared for the "big storm."

It took two days before the hurricane got to us. By then, the party atmosphere was over. It was hot, sticky, and muggy because all the power had gone off, including air conditioning, of course! I was so tired of waiting for the big event that I slept through most of it. That is, until water started pouring in my front door, the two back doors almost blew off their hinges, and an awning over my office blew away!

After the hurricane left, there were a million pieces of tree limbs and leaves and trash to pick up. Now when a hurricane is coming, I leave!

Good reading and good weather,

Carole Marsh

Christina "Mystery Girl" Mimi Papa Grant

Hey, kids! As you see, here we are ready to embark on another of our exciting Carole Marsh Mystery adventures. My grandchildren often travel with me all over the world as I research new books. We have a great time together, and learn things we will carry with us for the rest of our lives!

I hope you will go to www.carolemarshmysteries.com and explore the many Carole Marsh Mysteries series!

Well, the *Mystery Girl* is all tuned up and ready for "take-off!" Gotta go...Papa says so! Wonder what I've forgotten this time?

Happy "Armchair Travel" Reading,

Mimi

ABOUT THE CHARACTERS

Artemis Masters is an absentminded genius. He's a scientist at the top of his field in the early detection of natural disasters. Everyone looks to him to solve the mysteries of nature…he just needs someone to find his car keys, shoes and glasses!

Curie Masters, though only 12, has inherited her father's intelligence and ability to see things others don't. She has a natural penchant to solve mysteries…even if it means tangling with those older and supposedly smarter than her.

Nick Masters, an 8-year-old boy who's tall enough to pass as 12, likes to match wits with his sister and has her desire to solve mysteries others overlook. While he's the younger sibling, he tends to want to protect his sister, and of course, be the first to solve the mystery.

BOOKS IN THIS SERIES:

TABLE OF CONTENTS

CHAPTER ONE

CRANKING UP THE POWER

"Crank it up to a Category 4!" eleven-year-old Curie yelled to Nick, her eight-year-old brother. Nick clicked the mouse, sending a signal to the computer-generated program that operated a small-scale wind tunnel in their home's basement. Inside the wind tunnel was a small village of tiny houses and buildings, street signs, and cars. Some houses were constructed to withstand hurricane force winds.

"Here goes a Category 3," Nick shouted as the wind in the tunnel accelerated with a *whoosh*.

"The street signs are blowing over, Dad!" Curie yelled to her father.

"That's to be expected in a Category 3," their father Artemis said, giving an expert's view of the situation while his glasses slid off the end of his nose. "Curie, watch the buildings," he said. "Check the uplift, racking and sliding. That's what we really want to know—if there is structural damage to the buildings. And where did my glasses go?"

"Category 4!" Nick yelled, trying to be heard above the louder *whoosh* from the wind tunnel as he scooped up his father's glasses from the floor.

"Uplift—that's when wind blows through and over the house, lifting the roof right off the house," Curie said, trying to remember what she had learned. "It's not happening to the red, blue, or yellow house. But, wow! Look, the roof is coming off the white house!"

"That's the house without the Masters' ties and bindings holding the roof on," Artemis whooped as he put on his glasses, peering

through the thick lenses. "Even I can see my connectors are holding the houses together!"

"You can shut down the tunnel now, Nick," Artemis said. "We have some useful information to record."

"I was hoping you'd say that," Nick replied. "I don't want to totally destroy that little white house, Dad! I built it myself."

"Now you know how a homeowner might feel when he sees his roof being blown away!" Artemis said.

Curie piped up, "And a wild hurricane season is predicted for this summer. I hope your ties and bindings will protect a lot of people's houses from losing roofs, sliding off the foundations, and being bent sideways..."

"Racking is the precise word," Artemis corrected, as he adjusted his lopsided glasses to look at his daughter.

"OK, Dad, racking," Curie said, wrinkling her nose.

Artemis was a brilliant but absentminded scientist with an

expertise in seismic shift. The wind tunnel prototype was testing whether his specially designed, earthquake-proof steel fittings and bindings, located at the joints and within the frame of a house, could also work in hurricanes. If they did, the fittings and bindings could provide double protection for a home. For this reason, Artemis was hired as a consultant for *Build 'Em Strong, Inc.*, a company that reinforced existing buildings. The kids knew he would lead two teams inspecting the homes where the Masters' ties and bindings had been recently installed. If a hurricane struck one or more of these homes, Artemis and the teams would report on how well his design worked.

Curie and Nick badly wanted to go with their dad on an investigation trip so they helped him build and test his wind tunnel, and learned everything they could about hurricanes.

Nick decided it was time to bring the subject up with their dad. "See, Dad," he said, "Curie knows a lot about how winds affect

a house. We're on summer vacation. Do you think we could go with you on one of your trips?"

Artemis laughed. His plan of roping in the interest of his kids had worked! He said in a very serious voice, "Are you, Curie and Copernicus Masters, up to taking a long trip with me to see if my ties and bindings will work in real houses?"

"Wow!" Nick yelled, knowing that when their father used their full names he was talking serious science. After all, they were named after famous scientists and wanted to be scientists when they grew up. "That would be better than summer camp!"

"And maybe we can learn all about hurricanes firsthand," Curie said. "I presume we're going where there are lots of hurricanes!"

"There's a good chance we'll see one up close," Artemis replied. "We'll be driving to the Florida and Gulf coasts. Those places get

hit by hurricanes a lot. It's a long drive. Are you sure you want to go?"

Watching his kids gyrate around him like Cherokee war dancers was answer enough.

"We'll be leaving in a few days. Start packing," Artemis said. "You know the routine for everything that needs to go into the van.

"Also," Artemis added, "get acquainted with the investigation team's website and blogs. I got permission for you two to access the site."

"Did you tell them we're interns, and not just your kids?" Curie asked.

"I did," Artemis replied.

"Thank goodness Nick's tall for his age," Curie said. She couldn't resist needling her smart brother. "He can pass for 12 if he watches out for me like a big brother, instead of teasing me like little brothers do!"

"Ha!" said Nick. "You know I always watch out for you because you need lots of help!"

"Enough of that," Artemis said as he handed Curie a piece of paper. "Here are the passwords, user IDs, and website. Go online and check it out. Learn all you can about the project and feel free to blog. You might tell them that our experiment today worked!"

The kids quickly huddled over Nick's laptop computer, learning about the teams' activities and plans. Nick loved to blog so he moved to the section of the site reserved for blogging. Dozens of blogging topics had been set up by the company and team members. It would be easy to get lost in all of them. Nick noticed that whole blogging conversations could go on in secret. He clicked on a link and glanced over a blog entitled "Categories." An entry from a person using the name RedRooster read, *TruckingCharlie, are you taking the Category 2's to the storage point we indicated?*

TruckingCharlie replied, *I can, but it could be dicey.*

Nick asked Curie to look at the blog. "What do you suppose this means?" he asked.

"It's strange," she replied, "but we'll have to find out what it means later. We have to pack!"

Little did the kids know this strange blog would introduce them to as much danger as this season's biggest hurricane!

CHAPTER TWO:

THE TIES THAT BIND

"Hey Curie, do you think this shirt makes me look like a little kid?" Nick asked, as he combed his hair in front of the mirror.

"No, it's better than the one with little boats all over it!" Curie yelled, looking through the bathroom door. Both kids were taking more than the usual care with their dress today. They wanted to look like real interns and not just some kids tagging along because there was no babysitter.

There was a knock on the door. Artemis yelled from the front room, "I'll get the door. Nick, make sure everyone has a seat when they arrive. Curie, could you please see to the snacks?"

Artemis led the investigation team members of *Build 'Em Strong, Inc.* into the living room. There were five men in each of the two groups. They were meeting at the Masters' house to kick off the inspection trip, discuss trip plans and get work assignments.

After Curie and Nick were introduced, the kids tried to perform their host functions like adults. Nick solemnly pulled up a chair for one of the guests. "Please sit here," he said before the chair got caught on a rug. The man's bottom was already on its way down, and didn't find the chair! Instead, he landed with a thud on the rug.

"Here, let me help!" Curie cried, dumping a bag of greasy chips on another guest's lap as she jumped up to assist the fallen man.

Artemis quickly got up to wipe the chips from his guest's pants. As Artemis leaned

forward to help, the glasses on his nose slid off and plopped into the guest's iced tea while the glasses hanging around his neck smacked the guest on the chin—a double whammy!

"We don't often entertain," Curie said, embarrassed. "But we are glad you're here!" She dashed off to get another iced tea as Artemis fished his glasses out of his guest's drink.

Feeling like little kids who couldn't do anything, Curie and Nick sat on the sidelines, not saying much. After these mess-ups, they at least wanted to *look* smart. They decided to **defer** to the adults by not debating their opinions but just listening to their conversation.

"*Hurricane Katrina* in 2005 was a real wakeup call for everybody," said Red, a tall, thin man in jeans. "It was the worst hurricane in U.S. history in terms of damage. Taxpayers will need to spend more than $100 billion to make it all right. Hundreds of thousands of homes were destroyed in

New Orleans and along the Gulf Coast. We've had no problem convincing homeowners to strengthen their homes with Artemis' ties and bindings."

Curie and Nick looked at each other, wide-eyed. It was hard to imagine such a catastrophe.

Artemis began the meeting by suggesting that everyone get connected to the website. There, they would find any necessary documents and information.

"My kids are avid bloggers," Artemis said. "They tell me that you are already making use of the blogs. That's great. It's important that we stay in touch!"

Red scratched his head. "Some of the blogs we'd like to keep, uh, private—nothing to hide, mind you," he remarked with a twisted frown. "It's just that my team sometimes uses rough language. I wouldn't want your kids exposed to things they don't need to see."

Artemis laughed. "Hear that, kids?" Artemis said. "You got fair warning."

Nick and Curie again glanced at each other, remembering the weird blog they read the night before. It didn't have any "rough language."

As the men talked, Curie observed the members of the two teams. One team was led by an older, gray-haired man named Oscar. He was silent and thoughtful. His team members were rowdy young men, always joking with each other. They seemed to know one another very well. The other team was led by Red. His team seemed to be divided. Two guys hung out together and another pair, who appeared to be brothers, stuck to themselves.

Artemis and the men discussed the trip. It was decided that Artemis and the kids would meet up with the teams on certain dates to inspect the houses.

"So we do go back to a house that's been hit by a hurricane—even if the owner has evacuated to another location?" Red asked.

"Yes," Artemis said. "It's important we see the house as soon as possible after a storm. The owners have to sign a release saying we have rights to inspect the house, even if they haven't returned to the house."

Red smiled a strange smile and looked at Oscar. His actions made Curie feel uncomfortable, along with the strange comment about not wanting Curie and Nick to see the "Categories" blogs. Was Red "RedRooster?" Should her father be mixed up with these people? Most of the team members seemed normal and professional. Or was she just worrying too much, getting the jitters before the start of a big trip?

CHAPTER THREE:

AN ILL WIND BLOWS

Finally, departure day came. "Pilot to co-pilot. All systems go?" Artemis asked, keeping with family tradition at the beginning of a big trip when everyone was buckled in, ready to "rock and roll."

"Roger that, captain," Curie answered on cue. "All systems are A-OK. Kick the tires and light the fires!"

Artemis hit the accelerator and the rickety old Masters of Disasters van rolled out of the driveway, on the road to this next adventure.

"Are we going to Louisiana first?" Nick asked.

"Yep, that's the plan," Artemis replied. "*Hurricane Katrina* was very destructive there so people want stronger houses. It'll be a long trip. Sit back and enjoy the scenery."

As the kids became bored, Artemis decided to test their hurricane knowledge. He knew they loved to compete with each other.

"We all know a hurricane has really strong winds, but tell me more, please? What is a hurricane?" Artemis asked.

"A hurricane is a large storm characterized by high winds rotating around a low pressure area called the eye," Nick piped up. "The winds must be blowing more than 74 miles an hour. Anything less is called a tropical storm."

"An average hurricane is 500 miles wide and can move at about 20 miles per hour—like a great spinning top," Curie added.

"Great!" said Artemis. "Now tell me how hurricanes are formed. Do they just come out of the blue?"

"Oh Dad," Curie fussed, shaking her head. "Of course not. Three conditions are needed. That's why we don't have hurricanes in the middle of winter."

"Well," Artemis asked, "What are they?"

"First," Curie held up one finger, "you need warm ocean water..."

"At least 26 degrees Celsius, or 79 degrees Fahrenheit," Nick interrupted.

"Ahem!" Curie griped. "Let me continue. Seventy-nine degrees is pretty warm, almost like a bathtub. The warm, moist air rising up from the water heats the cooler air above it, creating a low pressure area. Trade winds flow to this area, spiraling around it..."

"And a rotation of winds starts!" Nick interrupted, trying to get in the last word.

"And don't forget that the rotation of the earth also causes the winds to rise and twist, causing a cylinder to form," Artemis added.

"Dad," Curie fumed with frustration, "you stole my second condition for a hurricane. The third condition is the latitude where all this takes place. Hurricanes form between the 5th and 30th latitudes."

Since Nick was trying to act so smart, Curie decided to ask him a tough question. "Hey, Nick," she asked, "what are the four ways to detect a hurricane?"

Nick had to think a moment on that one. "Well, you can go into the ocean on a ship and find one," he replied.

"Easy to say but hard to do—it is a big ocean," Curie said. "But it is one way."

"A second way would be to fly a plane and hunt for one," Nick added.

"A little faster, but you might run out of gas looking," Curie said. "Still, it is another way."

"Satellites!" Nick whooped. "They can spot hurricanes from space and send the photos and position to earth."

"Right on," Curie replied. "And the last way?"

Nick scratched his head.

"Shall I give you a clue?" Curie suggested.

"You and your clues," Nick moaned, not wanting to admit he needed one.

"Weathermen always talk about it on the weather report when there is a storm," Curie remarked.

"Doppler radar!" Nick answered.

"Not bad," said Artemis. "Anybody know the difference between a hurricane and typhoon?"

"Typhoons," Nick answered, "are hurricanes that form in the Pacific Ocean."

"You're right," Artemis said. "Typhoons start west of the International Date Line, which is located in the Pacific Ocean. Typhoons hit places like Japan and China. Hurricanes start east of the International Date Line."

Artemis decided to toss out one more test of hurricane knowledge. "I know you're both familiar with how the strength of hurricanes is rated," he said.

Curie jumped in immediately. "Category 1 to 5, with a Cat 5 being the worst," she declared.

"Correct," Artemis said, "but do you know what that rating system is called?"

"OH!" Curie cried. "It's on the tip of my tongue. It's S-something, like Sandler...Saucer...Sawyer..."

"The Saffir-Simpson Scale!" Nick shouted. He pumped his fist in the air in triumph.

"Good one, little brother," Curie said, gracefully accepting defeat.

Artemis turned on the van radio. The weather forecast mentioned that a tropical storm was brewing off the coast of Africa in the Atlantic Ocean, thousands of miles away. *Little did Artemis and the kids know that this storm was destined to grow into a monster Category 5 hurricane headed their way!*

CHAPTER FOUR:

TRAILER TALES

"Are we there yet?" Curie complained after several days on the road.

"It's only about an hour to New Orleans," Artemis said, as the van passed the Lumberton exit on U.S. Interstate 59 going south to Slidell, Louisiana.

"Dad, Curie, look to the right!" Nick yelled. "I've never seen such a huge trailer park. It's a trailer metropolis!"

As the car got closer, Artemis and the kids could see that no one was living in the trailers. Hundreds of empty trailers just sat in a huge empty lot. It looked eerie.

"I don't see any banners so I don't think they're for sale. Dad, what are those trailers doing there?" Nick asked.

"I heard that the government is collecting the trailers that housed people temporarily when their homes were damaged by *Katrina*," Artemis replied. "It looks like this is a collection point of some kind for the FEMA trailers."

Nick gulped. "Wow, there are so many of them," he said.

Artemis continued, "Well, over a year after *Katrina*, there were 30,000 families still living in FEMA trailers like those. But as families repair their homes or move into some other dwelling, the trailers are no longer needed. Maybe they end up here."

"Dad, what is FEMA?" Curie asked.

"FEMA stands for Federal Emergency Management Agency," Artemis answered. "That is the government agency responsible for handling major disasters. It provided trailers like these to people made homeless by *Katrina*."

Coming from the north, this was the first sign the Masters family saw of the disaster called *Hurricane Katrina*.

"Imagine trying to live in one of those trailers for a long time. It might seem fun or novel for a day or two, but for months on end..." Artemis said thoughtfully.

"I would think there's no privacy," said Curie, who loved to spend quiet time in her room or in a hot bubble bath.

"You're right," Artemis said. "And I heard that as many as ten people lived in one trailer."

"It must be hard for a kid to do homework when everyone else is talking or running around," Curie noted. "And where would you keep a dog or cat?"

"But if you look on the bright side," Nick said, "the family that trailers together stays together."

Curie rolled her eyes. "Nick, you are always the optimist!" she said.

"It's important to look on the bright side," Artemis said. "I heard funny stories of how people are doing 'extreme makeovers' of their trailers. You've heard of people making over their clothes or houses. Well, down here they have trailer makeovers because they are so plain and dull with beige vinyl wallpaper, and false wood for the tabletops."

"What do they do, Dad?" Curie asked.

"They create collages of family photos to hang on the walls and sew new covers for the foldout couch," Artemis said. "Some people make a joke of it all by decorating the bedroom to look like it belongs to a Hollywood movie star with plush white rugs on the floor and satin bedspreads on the bed!"

"I would hang my baseball posters on the walls," Nick said. "That would make the trailer seem like home to me."

The Masters found a cozy motel in Slidell. The kids were soon on their computers, **immersed** in reading email. Later, Curie couldn't resist going to the blog called "Categories." She was shocked when she read it. The user named RedRooster had written:

RedRooster
Watch what you say, those two nosy Masters kids will probably stick their noses where they don't belong.

Curie blushed, feeling like she was caught in the act. But what conversation needed watching? She didn't think it was rough language—except for the tacky reference to her and Nick, the content was certainly "clean" enough. *What was going on?*

CHAPTER FIVE:

KEEPING THE PEACE

The next day, the Masters left Slidell and rolled down I-10 into New Orleans. After crossing Lake Pontchartrain, the kids could immediately see that something monstrous had devastated east New Orleans. Mile after mile stood abandoned houses, shopping centers, and townhouses with broken windows, torn roofs, and stripped siding. Signs hung at odd angles. But here and there, amid all the destruction, a family had returned to their home to clean up and begin again.

Curie was stunned. "They surely must be brave to come back to this horror and try again," she observed.

Nick gulped. "It must be scary at night by themselves in a neighborhood of empty houses," he said. "Those people remind me of pioneers in the wilderness, carving out a piece of civilization!"

"It's been nearly two years since *Katrina*," Artemis remarked. "I'm sure a lot has been done to fix things up, but this area looks like almost nothing has been done!"

The Masters drove on in awed silence to Metairie, a town on the west side of New Orleans that suffered some flooding and wind damage from *Katrina*. The Masters were happy to see that this town had almost fully recovered. The only reminders of the hurricane were a few FEMA trailers sitting in front of homes not yet repaired.

In Metairie, Artemis screeched into a parking space in front of a Cajun restaurant. "We have a lunch date," he said. "We're meeting my friend David Logan, a local policeman. He can fill us in on what's happening around here."

The Masters feasted on gumbo and crawfish, which kept slipping off Nick's fork. He changed his tactics when he saw how David

ate them, by picking them up with his fingers. "Love these mudbugs!" Nick muttered.

As everyone was digging into their food, Curie said, "Mr. Logan, Dad said you were right in the thick of the *Katrina* disaster, working for weeks on end!"

"Yeah," David said, "I lived at the police station and slept in my car for two weeks."

"Were you too busy to go home?" Nick asked. He thought he had to work hard at school but he couldn't imagine working 24 hours a day for two weeks!

"That, and the fact I couldn't drive through the flood waters to get home," David said. "I was on the job when the hurricane hit."

"What caused the flooding? Did a levee break around here?" Artemis asked.

"That happened in New Orleans," David answered. "Here it was a matter of the pump operators not working the city pumps to remove the excess water. The canals emptying into Lake Pontchartrain backed up, and with the heavy rain, the town filled up like a bowl."

"Why were the pump operators not working?" Curie asked.

"For their own protection, they were let go to see to the safety of their families," David answered grimly.

"When were you able to finally get home?" Artemis asked.

"The flood waters subsided after about two weeks," David replied. "By that time, the water inside the house also drained out but left a terrific stench with mud and mold all over the place."

"How did you take a shower? At the police station?" asked Curie, who shuddered at the thought of not being clean.

"There was no water there for that," David said. "What we had, we saved for drinking. I didn't take a shower for two weeks. It was summer, too, so you can imagine what I smelled like!"

"I would know," Curie said, eyeing Nick. "Sometimes I could bet Nick's gone almost two *years* without a shower!"

"Ha!" Nick said. "I do shower when I think of it. I am just into sports, so I sweat a lot!"

Nick quickly changed the subject. "What did you eat?" he asked.

"Well, all the restaurants and supermarkets were closed," David replied. "We had some rations and those ran out. Then, some thieves hijacked our ration delivery truck. We were forced to forage at the local supermarket, along with a lot of other people."

"Looting?" Nick asked, astonished.

David paused. "I wouldn't call it looting if you take what you need to survive—like food and first aid supplies," he finally answered. "But there was looting of the other kind. People took things like TVs and computers from the stores."

"Did people take stuff from the homes of people who left to escape the storm?" Curie wondered.

David said, "I personally didn't see the problem here, but that's often a serious problem after a hurricane. It certainly happened elsewhere."

When Curie heard this, it made her feel very uncomfortable. For some strange reason, her mind jumped to the odd messages she had read in the "Categories" blog on the team's website.

Curie and Nick pounced on their computers as soon as they returned to the van. Curie couldn't resist sending an email to RedRooster saying that she didn't see any rough language. She asked what the topic of the "Categories" blog really was. If it was something she or Nick shouldn't be reading, the kids would gladly oblige by respecting their privacy.

RedRooster quickly replied by email to Curie. He said the blog was just discussing moving supplies and storing them in trailers, and he'd prefer the kids didn't read it because his team could get nasty. *Was this a hidden warning? Was there a connection between the policeman's discussion of looting and the messages they had seen on the "Categories" blog?*

CHAPTER SIX

A BLAST FROM THE PAST

"Next stop—Waveland, Mississippi," said Artemis, the wind whipping his red hair as the van barreled down the highway. Waveland was the home of his friend, Ida Mae Jennings. She had invited Artemis and the kids to see where her house had once been, and to ask Artemis about his ties and bindings meant to strengthen houses.

As the family neared Waveland, they noticed something different. There were fewer damaged homes here. In fact, there were simply no homes standing at all. The area had been wiped out!

Artemis asked his kids a hurricane question. "Why do you suppose Waveland got hit harder than Metairie, where we just were?"

The kids thought about it a minute and couldn't come up with an answer.

"It's because Waveland got hit from the east side of the hurricane," Artemis said. "That's its fiercest side.   There is an expression, 'East is beast, west is best.' That means it's better to be on the west side of a hurricane because a hurricane moves counterclockwise in the northern hemisphere, thrusting its biggest punch on the east side."

As they drove along the road running parallel to the beach, there was not a single house standing on the opposite side from the ocean. Only the foundations sketched the outlines of the houses that once stood here.

Artemis saw his old friend, Ida Mae, waving from her damaged lot.

As Artemis pulled into her driveway, he hurriedly informed his kids, "Remember, this is the South. You are to address older women as 'ma'am.' Do you hear me?"

"Yes, Dad," Curie said, "we'll sound like uncultured dopes if we don't."

Ida Mae, the ocean breeze blowing her sunbonnet and dress, gave Artemis big hug. "Artemis, it's been ages!" Ida Mae cried in a warm Southern accent. "I haven't seen you since I retired from the Army. Not since we worked on that research project...and look! Now you have two great kids!"

Artemis pulled the children toward him. "My daughter's name is Curie," he said proudly.

"Hello, ma'am," Curie said, a little awed at meeting a woman who was once a high-ranking Army officer.

"And, Nick here," Artemis said, as he pulled a suddenly shy Nick to the front, "Nick is my son."

"Hi, madam," Nick stammered, embarrassed at his mistake, "I...I... mean ma'am."

Ida Mae laughed. "Artemis, I can see that you've trained them well. But they aren't from the South!"

"No ma'am," Nick said, now getting the hang of it.

"But I'll bet you still go for chocolate chip cookies and lemonade like Southern kids," Ida Mae said as she pointed toward a table graced with a blue-and-white checked tablecloth topped with goodies.

"Yes, ma'am!" Nick piped up with great gusto.

As the group sat down, Ida Mae said, "This was once my porch. You can see how big my house was by looking at the cement foundation." She pointed to the cement slab forming a big rectangle on the ground, now overgrown with weeds, driftwood, and debris.

"I remember you sent me pictures of a beautiful garden—bushes and shrubs, a lawn, the whole bit," Artemis commented.

"All that got washed or blown away!" Ida Mae said sadly, looking out at the wide sandy beach across the street from her house. "The insurance company thinks the house actually got blown away by a tornado before the storm surge came up over the road."

"A tornado!" Nick cried in disbelief, almost choking on a cookie.

"Tornadoes often form around the edges of a hurricane," Artemis said. "That's one more deadly feature of a hurricane."

"When the storm surge came, it was about twenty feet high," Ida Mae added. "That would have finished the job in any case. Except for my mother's silverware, which ended up in the backyard, everything else went northwest. My motor boat landed in a tree two blocks away!"

Artemis noticed his kids were stunned to the

point of silence. He asked them, "Do you know what a storm surge is?"

"That's when the high winds push the water to the shore, causing a surge of water to run up the beach on to land," Nick answered.

"You have smart kids, Artemis," Ida Mae said. "Are you training them to be scientists?"

"Of course; they're helping me as interns on a project now," Artemis said proudly.

The kids excused themselves and made a dash for the beach. They chased and splashed each other in the shallow surf while Ida Mae and Artemis talked about using Artemis' ties and bindings to strengthen her new beach house when it was built.

After the kids returned, Ida Mae expressed concern about the Masters' own hurricane preparedness. "Where will you go if a hurricane strikes?" Ida Mae asked. "There's a nasty tropical storm building up now in the Atlantic."

"So I've heard," Artemis said.

"If you need a place to stay," Ida Mae cautioned, "don't try the hotels. They'll be filled. You all just come to my safe house. After *Katrina*, I bought a house fifty miles north of here to ride out hurricanes. It's not too fancy but there's plenty of room."

"That's very kind of you," Artemis said, raising his lemonade glass. "Here's hoping it won't be necessary."

Curie was glad Ida Mae made the offer. She had a feeling they would need it.

CHAPTER SEVEN:

INSPECTING THE INSPECTION SUSPECTS

Waving goodbye to Ida Mae, the Masters drove east to Bay St. Louis, another town that was badly damaged by *Katrina*. There were many signs that the town was coming back to life. Businesses were open, the sounds of saws and hammers rang out on the streets, and traffic was more than just passersby gawking at the destruction.

Artemis and the kids met up with Oscar and his team at a new home that had just been fitted with Artemis' ties and bindings.

Artemis knocked on the door and a middle-aged man opened it. A big, fluffy golden retriever stuck his nose out to greet Artemis, who immediately fell into a sneezing fit. "ACHOO! ACHOO!   This is...ACHOO!...my   team,"   he   stammered. "Excuse me, I am...ACHOO!...allergic to dogs! I can't be around them, but they always seem to love me!"

"I'm Earl," the man said, "and this pup here is Sammy. Let me put him in his pen in the back yard."

Earl trotted back from the dog pen and invited the team into the house. "Am I glad to see you, Mr. Masters," he said. "I hope you can tell me if the contractor properly installed the reinforcements."

"That's   why   we're   here,"   Artemis replied. "In case another hurricane comes, we would also like to return after the storm to document how the ties and bindings worked."

"We get plenty of hurricanes," Earl said. "But hopefully you won't have to come back—at least in my lifetime!

Earl showed the team around the outside of his house, pointing out where the fittings and connectors were installed. Where visible, the team inspected the metal ties. Team members also made notes about the ties and bindings, such as where they were applied, how many, and what type were used.

Then Earl led the team into the attic to show how the connectors held the roof to the house. When they came back downstairs, he offered them some iced tea flavored with mint leaves. Since it was a typical, hot southern day, no one refused.

As they gulped down their tea, a member of Oscar's team, Jake, commented on Earl's coin collection in the living room.

Jake, it seemed, was also interested in coins. He asked lots of questions. As Earl enthusiastically described how valuable some of the rare coins were, Curie thought it would be easy to know what valuables were in a person's home by doing these inspections. The team could see everything that wasn't hidden away. And Earl was so trusting to tell them about his treasures!

It was Curie's role to enter Oscar's team notes into the computer. As she did so that night, her mind nagged her with an uncomfortable question. Why was Jake so interested in Earl's possessions?

The next day, Artemis and the kids met up with Red and his team in the town of Gulfport. Again, they went through the procedures of meeting the homeowner, and doing the inspections outside and inside the house. And once again, the homeowner, Mrs. Worth, invited the team to have iced tea and cake.

Curie listened closely as a member of Red's team asked Mrs. Worth about a massive seascape painting hanging in her living room.

It was a painting anyone living on the Gulf Coast would appreciate and want.

Mrs. Worth was only too happy to talk about it, saying it was done by a famous local artist. She said with a triumphant smile, "The artist's work is now worth thousands of dollars a painting. Of course, I got this for pennies when he was a starving artist, just starting out."

Curie noted again this was a chance to find out what was of value in a person's home.

That evening, it was Nick's chore to type in the findings of Red's team. He went to the van to get the computer. The computer wasn't there. He thought Curie had taken it into the motel room where they were staying.

"Hey Curie, did you bring in my laptop?" Nick asked.

"Nope," Curie replied. "The last time I saw it, it was in the van—before we went into Mrs. Worth's house."

Nick asked Artemis if he knew where it was. Artemis hadn't seen it, either.

"Dad, that laptop wasn't just sitting out in the open in the van. Somebody had to know where it was," Nick remarked.

"Let's go back to the van and look again," Artemis suggested.

Artemis, Nick and Curie pulled everything out of the van to search it thoroughly. As Nick removed a box, a piece of torn paper with writing on it fluttered to the floor.

"Look what I found," Nick cried as he held up the paper. He read:

Now, Curie had more troubling questions. Did someone leave this note and steal the computer when they were inspecting Mrs. Worth's house, or sometime shortly afterwards?

So many things smelled fishy, and the smell wasn't coming from the Gulf beach just across the road from their motel.

CHAPTER EIGHT:

THE UNSINKABLE MOLLY BROWN

The next inspection site was in Biloxi, Mississippi. Artemis, the kids, and Oscar's inspection team visited an elderly lady, Mrs. Beckwith. She had survived *Hurricane Camille*, a Category 5 hurricane that struck the Gulf Coast in August of 1969. Until *Katrina*, *Camille* was probably the worst hurricane in U.S. history in terms of property damage.

Mrs. Beckwith was a lively old woman with white curly hair. She had a white poodle with curly hair much like her own that yapped at everyone. She called the dog Dixie, and was obviously very attached to it, holding it close and petting its head. The dog leaned forward and licked Artemis on the nose.

Artemis began his bouts of sneezing. With one big "ACHOO!" his glasses went flying, glancing off the dog's head, and sending Dixie into a yapping fit to match his sneezing fit. Artemis apologized. "I....ACHOO!...am allergic ...ACHOO!...to dogs!"

Between the sneezing and the barking, not much could be said so Mrs. Beckwith locked the dog in another room. Artemis blew his nose, and calmed down enough to introduce the lady to his team. Mrs. Beckwith led the team on an outside tour of the house. The home was a work of art. It was one of those old Southern mansions built before the Civil War with large white pillars lining the front porch. Artemis could see it was built to last a long time and had probably survived numerous hurricanes.

Mrs. Beckwith brought the team inside and up to the attic. The team saw that her house had been strongly reinforced all the way

around with Artemis' ties and bindings. Artemis was glad to tell her that her house would survive a strong hurricane.

"I'm delighted," Mrs. Beckwith said. "I've heard a well-built attic is the best place to be if there is flooding. It's as high as you can go—and you can still escape through the roof. See, I installed a skylight that opens up!"

Mrs. Beckwith led the team downstairs to the living room. The chatty old lady, who loved the company, served lemonade and immediately launched into her *Hurricane Camille* survival story.

Curie noticed that Oscar was eyeing the wide-screen, high-definition TV that seemed to occupy half the wall. Curie told herself to not be so suspicious of other people. She was soon caught up in Mrs. Beckwith's story.

"I was much younger back then," Mrs. Beckwith said, as if it needed mentioning. "I could swim very far. And it was a good thing. It saved my life."

"What happened?" Artemis asked.

"I wasn't living here then," Mrs. Beckwith began. "I had a house close to the beach. I thought I could ride out the storm. It's so hard to leave one's home and camp out with relatives. Well, the waters kept coming and coming. The house held, but just barely. I could it hear it creak and groan as the floor shifted. I watched as the water rose to my waist, with a fish swimming near me. So I swam to the stairs and pulled myself upstairs to my bedroom on the second floor. The water still kept rising. I didn't have an attic in that house. I was on my knees praying, I can tell you."

Mrs. Beckwith took a deep breath and shifted in her chair. "Then," she said, "magically, the water stopped rising. I thought I was safe. But when the water receded back to the ocean, the house gave way, washing out to sea with the current. I was carried away with the house as it broke apart, sinking under water. I managed to swim through the

breaking debris and up to the surface. I found what had been my front door and climbed on board. I floated for a while and decided I had better paddle to the beach while I could still see the shore. I actually made it!"

"You are a true 'Unsinkable Molly Brown!'" Artemis exclaimed. "Like the tough lady who survived the *Titanic* disaster!"

Mrs. Beckwith grinned from ear to ear. "You know that story! People do call me the 'Unsinkable Molly Brown!'" she said, nodding her head.

The team stood up to make their departure. Mrs. Beckwith thanked everyone for visiting. The group was quiet as they walked out, thoroughly awed by little old Mrs. Beckwith's story.

Curie and Nick were among the last to leave the house. Mrs. Beckwith had asked the children about their roles on the team. As Nick bounded down the steps to catch up with the others, a small slip of paper lying on the step caught his eye. Thinking it was something belonging to the team, he picked up the paper and stuffed it into his jeans pocket—and then forgot all about it.

That night, at their motel, Nick cleaned out his pockets and found the piece of paper. "Oh, yeah," he said. "I forgot about you." It was a list of some sort.

Nick showed the paper to Curie. "What do you think this is?" he asked. I found it on Mrs. Beckwith's step. I thought it was some note made by a team member."

Curie studied the paper. "It does look like a list," she said, "but it's not like any 'to do' or shopping list I've seen." She read:

Category 1 - G 55
Category 2 - B 124

What disturbed Curie was the repetition of the word "Category." That word was coming up all too much lately—in hurricanes, in blogs and now in this note.

CHAPTER NINE:

NOT MY NAME!

Their work on the project done for the day, Curie and her father took a dip in the motel swimming pool. With Nick's laptop missing, Nick had to share time on Curie's laptop. Now it was free for him to use. Also he felt tired—one more reason for choosing the **sedentary** activity of surfing the Internet.

He clicked the link to the National Hurricane Center's website and looked for something interesting to read. The headline on the home page jumped out at him, TROPICAL STORM *MARIE* NOW UPGRADED TO HURRICANE. Beneath the headline was a satellite image of the white pinwheel churning in the ocean. *Marie* was in the Atlantic moving west, just north of the Caribbean, rapidly gathering steam and heading for Florida!

Newly posted articles warned Floridians what to expect and how to prepare for the hurricane, now just a Category 1 but expected to grow stronger.

Nick clicked the television remote to watch the meteorologist announce the same thing he had read on the Internet. Feisty *Marie* was picking up speed.

When Artemis and Curie returned to the motel room, Nick said, "Remember that tropical storm we've been hearing about? It's now a hurricane. And guess what it's named?"

"Nick!" Curie said. "A perfect name for a hurricane!"

"No," said Nick, laughing, "A better name than that—one that's really suitable!"

"*Marie*?" Curie asked, knowing her brother was making a reference to her feisty attitude about things.

"You guessed it!" Nick said.

"NOT MY NAME!" Curie moaned. "If the storm morphs into a monster, nobody will name their daughters Marie! And people, when they hear my name, will remember that storm. Just like *Katrina*. Nobody names their daughters that now—especially in New Orleans."

Curie fumed, shaking her head. "Dad, how do hurricanes get named?" she asked.

"The World Meteorological Organization makes a list of names in alphabetical order for each year," Artemis answered. "The names alternate between men's and women's names."

"Didn't hurricanes used to be named after women only?" Nick asked.

"Yep, that's right," Artemis replied. "But it's not really fair to women, is it? Men can be just as unpredictable as women."

"Do they have a different list of names for typhoons in the Pacific?" Curie asked.

"Good question," Artemis said. "They do. And hurricanes that approach Hawaii are given Hawaiian names."

The family gathered around the TV to watch the local weather channel track the hurricane. They heard the forecaster say that *Marie* had upgraded to a Category 2. He also said that Florida was now on a hurricane watch.

"What does that mean, Dad?" Nick asked.

"It means there is a possibility that a hurricane could strike within 36 hours," Artemis said. "It's the trigger to start implementing disaster preparedness plans, and to secure large objects like boats."

"A hurricane warning must mean hurricane conditions are present," Nick added, thinking hard.

"Just about," Artemis replied. "A warning means that hurricane conditions will

occur within 24 hours and that you should determine the safest place to stay."

Later that night, when Artemis and Nick were asleep, Curie checked the weather report once more. *Marie* had been upgraded again! She was now a Category 3 and growing bigger and faster by the minute.

Curie realized here was a possible test for her father's ties and bindings. Houses might stand or fall, and lives might be saved or lost, depending on how well his specially designed reinforcements worked! She crossed her fingers for good luck.

CHAPTER TEN:

EENIE MEENIE MINEE MO — WHICH WAY WILL THE HURRICANE GO?

Over the next couple of days, *Hurricane Marie* made landfall in Florida as a Category 3, crossed over the middle part of the state, and blew into the Gulf of Mexico as a Category 2.

"Why did *Marie* lose steam? Nick asked his dad.

"Hurricanes lose their source of power, the ocean water, when they cross over land," Artemis replied. "*Marie* had nothing to feed on over land. But now that she's in the Gulf, she'll have plenty of warm water for fuel. She will be a very dangerous storm unless she turns north quickly."

As *Hurricane Marie* entered the Gulf, she swerved this way and that. Forecasters had a hard time predicting where she would go. She could make landfall anywhere from Florida to Texas. One thing was clear, however. *Marie* had gained power and became a Category 3 storm as she fed off the warm waters of the Gulf.

After staying at humdrum motels near the inspection sites, the Masters enjoyed a night of camping on the beach. They kept their radio closely tuned to hear the progress of the hurricane.

In the morning, it was clear that veterans of *Hurricane Katrina* were taking no chances. Nick watched as other people

camping at the beach loaded gear and supplies into their vehicles.

"Hey, look, Dad," Nick said as he loaded the camping equipment in the van. "People are moving out! Maybe we should get going?"

"It looks like it," Artemis said, "but I need to check on my teams first, and get a reading on whether our clients who have used my ties and fittings are leaving or staying."

Curie sometimes wondered at her father's obliviousness to danger, and this was one of those times. "Dad, we need to find a safe spot inland, especially if the hurricane heads in this direction! Do you have any plans?" Curie asked.

Artemis stood up and ran his hands through his spiky hair. "We'll find a place," he said. "Don't worry!"

This wasn't good enough for Curie, who liked to plan ahead. "Can I call your friend, Ida Mae Jennings, and ask her if we could take

up her offer to stay at her place?" she suggested.

"Oh, sure," Artemis said, slightly relieved that his bright daughter had come up with a solution he didn't want to think about at the moment.

Curie immediately called Ida Mae. She quickly arranged to stay at Ida Mae's safe house deep in the Mississippi woodlands, away from the coast.

While Artemis was on the phone with his teams, the kids hustled to the local supermarket to get supplies for a possible evacuation to Ida Mae's house. Artemis had given them a list of goods to buy.

As Curie and Nick entered the supermarket, they were shocked to see lines of 20 people deep at each cash register.

"Look, Curie," Nick said, "those people's shopping carts couldn't hold one more thing!"

"There's a run on bottled water and canned goods, that's for sure!" Curie commented. "That man's cart is loaded with five cases of water."

"It's a good thing we got here early!" Nick remarked, as the kids charged down the aisle to pick up bottled water.

The kids grabbed water and extra batteries for the radio and flashlight. They also bought some fresh fruit, canned goods, and bread. Because they were on a trip, they already had most of the other items usually included in an evacuation list, such as Dad's many glasses, medications, maps, keys, and important documents.

The kids returned to find Artemis at his command post in the van. He had already determined his teams' whereabouts and plans. He was now gathering information on who would stay and who would evacuate the houses inspected by the teams. So far, it looked like Earl, Mrs. Worth, and Mrs. Beckwith were making plans to escape if necessary.

"Curie," Atemis said, "can you let the teams know on the website blog that all the

people we visited plan to evacuate their homes?"

Nick and Curie looked at each other. They hadn't told their father about their suspicions or the strange blogs. At this hour, their father had so much on his mind. They didn't want to worry him further by bringing up their concerns.

"Sure, Dad," Curie replied, "but that's not a real priority right now, is it?

"No," Artemis said. "It can wait until we get to Ida Mae's. Besides, by then someone may have changed their mind about evacuating."

Nick put some fresh batteries into the radio and tuned to the Weather Channel. He heard that *Hurricane Marie* was now a Category 4 and was like a herd of wild horses galloping around a field, feeding off rich grain. He told Artemis and Curie the news. "It also says on the radio that the highways are filling with people evacuating north," he said.

"We don't want to get stuck on the major highways, and certainly not I-10, which goes east and west," Artemis said as he tossed a large atlas to Curie. "Don't just use the GPS device. Consult this map and plot a course to Ida Mae's that takes the state highways, first going northwest to Mississippi. Get to know all the side roads in the area. You never know if we might need to use one."

Since the Masters were now near Mobile, Alabama, Curie looked at the map and quickly saw that Highway 98 would take them northwest. From there they could take Highway 26 to arrive at Ida Mae's. She checked the route on the GPS, and told her father the plan.

"Great work, Curie," Artemis said. "You've completed your first evacuation plan. Now let's get the van gassed up."

The Masters stopped for lunch in a crowded restaurant near the gas station. The TV on the wall commanded everyone's attention because it was tuned to the local weather channel tracking the storm.

The forecaster announced that Hurricane Marie was now a whopping Category 5! And it was headed to Mobile, Alabama—right where Nick and Curie were eating their lunch!

CHAPTER ELEVEN:

WHEN FREEWAYS ARE PARKING LOTS

After wolfing down their lunches, the Masters joined the thousands in Mobile taking to the highways to flee *Hurricane Marie*. Artemis drove the evacuation route planned by Curie, taking Highway 98 out of Mobile. When they arrived at the I-65 intersection, it was clear that a major evacuation was underway. Cars were crawling along at a snail's pace.

"Dad, look," Nick yelled, "all the cars are in the northbound lane. Nobody is going south! Wow, does that look weird!"

"Maybe the police will open up some of the southbound lanes so people can use them to go north," Artemis commented. He turned on the radio just in time to hear the governor order an emergency evacuation for all persons living on the coast.

"It looks like everyone got the message!" Nick exclaimed.

Artemis asked Curie to call his clients and ask if they were still going to evacuate. No one answered. The last name on the list was Mrs. Beckwith, the dear old "Unsinkable Molly Brown."

The phone rang, and Curie's heart sank when she heard Mrs. Beckwith answer the line. She still hadn't left her home!

"Mrs. Beckwith, this is Curie Masters," said Curie. "My father wants to know if you plan to evacuate."

"Oh, my dear," Mrs. Beckwith said, "I had planned to, but I can't."

"Why?" Curie asked, a little worried.

"My dear poodle, Dixie," Mrs. Beckwith explained, "broke her leg this morning when she jumped off the couch. The vet is gone, and I can't take Dixie anywhere in her

condition. And I can't **forsake** her by leaving her here alone."

Curie turned to her father and told him the situation.

"Let me speak to her," Artemis said. He grabbed the cell phone. "Tell me what you have for a survival kit," he instructed, as he tried to listen, drive the van, and keep his glasses from sliding off his sweaty nose.

The radio announcer continued to make grim warnings about the effects of Category 5 hurricanes. Curie shuddered. When Artemis hung up, she asked him if Mrs. Beckwith would be able to ride out the hurricane at home.

"Actually, she can," Artemis said. "She's one prepared lady. She had everything on the hurricane survival list, like water, non-perishable foods, a can opener, flashlight, first aid kit, batteries...the whole bit!

"Her house isn't close to the ocean," Artemis continued. "It's well built, and even stronger now with my reinforcements. She's got as good a chance as anybody who chooses to stay."

"The sky sure is looking weird!" Nick exclaimed. "Look that those spooky clouds! And the wind is picking up, too!"

"Hush, let's hear the weather report!" Artemis said, gripping the steering wheel tightly as the wind buffeted the van.

"*Marie* has changed her course," the announcer stated. "She's now headed for landfall at Biloxi, Mississippi."

"Oh, no!" Curie cried. "That's aimed right at Mrs. Beckwith!"

"And right toward us!" Nick added. "It's like we're being chased by a hurricane! Isn't Miss Ida Mae's house north of Biloxi?"

"Yes, it is," Artemis said, "and we can check out my client's house right across the street while we're there, too!"

CHAPTER TWELVE:

THE STORM BREAKS

Nick and Curie had to lean into the gusting winds as they staggered to the front door of Ida Mae's house. She and her husband, Jimmy Ray, welcomed the Masters with an early, home-cooked supper.

By the time the meal was over, the winds howled and screeched, whipping tree branches against the house and windowpanes.

"We better get those last few windows boarded up," Jimmy Ray said, as he put down his napkin. Artemis and the kids jumped up to help him nail bulky plywood sheets to the windows.

"Help!" Nick yelled. The group turned to see Nick being pushed backward and

upward by the wind swirling under the plywood sheet he carried over his head.

"You always wanted to learn to fly!" Curie said, laughing. "Now's your chance!"

Artemis reached out and grabbed the board from Nick just before he became airborne.

Inside the boarded-up house, the rooms were eerily dark. Ida Mae turned on the lights. Outside, the wind and rain slammed against the roof and sides of the house. The two families huddled around the TV to watch the progress of the storm. The TV news announcer said there was a chance *Hurricane Marie* might change course just before making landfall.

Every now and then, Nick and Curie peered out the cracks between the boarded windows to watch tree branches, leaves, and garbage can lids fly like missiles across the yard. *CRAAACK!* A massive tree limb crashed across the neighbor's driveway, and rolled back and forth furiously in the wind.

About 8:30 p.m., the electricity shut off. The house was completely dark and completely quiet.

"Oh, no!" said Curie. "Now what do we do?"

"It's okay, honey," said Ida Mae. "I have everything we need." Ida Mae was prepared with candles and hurricane lamps, but the flickering flames cast wavering shadows which seemed to move like ghosts in synch with the outside winds.

Using her cell phone's last remaining charge, Curie tried calling Mrs. Beckwith to see how she was doing. Curie could not make contact! The phone at the other end was dead, with an announcement saying service had been temporarily suspended.

How she hoped Mrs. Beckwith was okay, and that her family and new friends would be safe, too!

CHAPTER THIRTEEN:

THE EYE OF THE STORM

RRRIIINNNGGG!!!   Jimmy Ray's cell phone made everyone jump. His face twisted into a frown when he ended the conversation.

"What's wrong?" Ida Mae asked.

"Davis Dam just broke," he said. "We could be in for some serious flooding."

"Hey, the noise outside is going away!" Nick yelled. "Maybe the worst is over!"

"That's the eye of the storm," Artemis stated matter-of-factly. "It's starting to pass over us now. It means the other half of the storm is yet to come."

When the wind stopped completely, Nick and Curie ventured outside into a strangely quiet night scene lit by a sliver of a moon. Tree limbs littered the ground. Big

sections of roof dangled from neighboring houses. Water silently rose in the street, creeping up the tires of cars parked along the curb.

"Curie, look over at the house across the street!" Nick hissed. "Two guys are taking something out of that house. Isn't that the house Dad wanted to inspect?"

"It is!" Curie cried. "Do you think they're looting—or are they just removing their valuables?"

Without street lamps, it was hard to see the dim figures. In a moment, the two men jumped into a van and slid away through the rising water. It was too late for the kids to recognize their faces, but not too late to read part of the writing on the side of the van, *Build 'Em...*

"The van must belong to Dad's company, *Build 'Em Strong!*" Nick shouted.

"Some people in the company *are* looting—like we thought!" Curie concluded.

WHOOOOOSH! A blast of wind knocked Nick and Curie into each other, indicating the other side of the storm had arrived. They charged indoors, to find Ida Mae and Jimmy Ray anxiously peering through a crack, watching the water overflowing the road and creeping their way!

CHAPTER FOURTEEN:

A FLOOD OF CHALLENGES

Filthy brown water began pouring into Ida Mae's living room and kitchen despite the attempts of Jimmy Ray, Ida Mae, and Artemis to stuff the cracks under the doors with towels. Water gushed relentlessly through every opening. Nick stood frozen, awed by a dead fish floating in Ida Mae's living room. His trance was broken by Jimmy Ray firmly grabbing his arm.

"We've got to go higher," Ida Mae stated emphatically. "We don't have a second floor, but we do have a small attic," she added, pulling a cord from the ceiling that brought down a ladder. "The kids need to climb up there to get out of this polluted water!"

Nick and Curie scrambled up the ladder. They watched from the hot, steamy attic as the adults lost their battle with the rising tide. Knee deep in water, they began passing up candles, food, bottled water, and Artemis' laptop. They grimly joined the kids in a close huddle in the tiny attic. Jimmy Ray and Artemis wiped away the sweat pouring down their faces. Everyone watched silently as the water crept up the attic steps, wondering when it would stop.

Curie whispered to Nick, "Do you think we'll have to swim out, like the 'Unsinkable Molly Brown?'"

"I hope not," Nick replied. "We can always hang on to those rafters if we have to!"

After what seemed like hours, Jimmy Ray peered into the darkness below the attic opening. "I think the water has stopped risin'," he said in his thick Southern drawl.

"Oh, thank goodness!" Ida Mae sighed, as she leaned against the wall.

Even though it was now very late, sleep was impossible with the flood waters gushing around in the rooms below them, making the walls groan. Pounding rain and ripping winds tore at the roof.

Would the house hold together?

CHAPTER FIFTEEN

WHAT A MESS!

The next morning, the winds had died and the water had receded, leaving a muddy mess in Ida Mae's house and deep pools in the yard and street outside. Debris covered the ground in every direction.

Artemis powered up his laptop and made a wireless connection to the Internet after several attempts. He sent an email to his company letting them know where he and the kids were. Now it was time to get down to business and see how his invention had worked.

Curie couldn't get her mind off what she had seen the night before. "Dad," she asked, "can I use your computer?"

"Just for a minute," Artemis said. "We need to save the energy in the battery." Curie couldn't resist going to the "Categories" blog. The kids were stunned to see a list they recognized:

CATEGORY 1 - G 55
CATEGORY 2 - B 124

Nick and Curie looked at one another. "What if 'Category' stands for 'supplies' like Red said," Curie asked Nick, "and what if supplies means categories of stolen goods? What if G 55 represents a place or an address? Did anyone we visited have a street address with 55 in it?"

"No," Nick whispered, "but I know Mrs. Beckwith lives at 124 Bainbridge!"

"If B stands for the street where Mrs. Beckwith lives," Curie whispered back, "then these might be places that are targeted for looting!"

"Dad, we need to tell you something!" Curie said. "We think some of the team members are looting the houses we inspect!"

"What did you say?" Artemis hollered, not believing his ears. "Has this storm gone to your heads?"

Curie recounted her suspicions from the beginning, starting with the strange messages on the "Categories" blog, the lack of rough language on the blog despite what Red said, the stolen laptop, the team's interest in the clients' personal possessions, and the event across the street last night. Listening in, Ida Mae noted that the house across the street was #55 and that their street was Greenway. That fit the list pattern!

"Let's all visit the house across the street," Artemis said. "I can't wait to see how it withstood the storm. We'll look around the inside for signs of theft, too."

A quick examination of the house proved the strength of Artemis' ties and bindings. But Artemis and the kids couldn't tell for sure if anything had been stolen.

"Can we check on Mrs. Beckwith and Dixie?" Curie asked. "I haven't been able to reach her. And we think her house is targeted for looting!"

"Sure, if we can get to her house," Artemis replied. "Many roads are impassable. Since Oscar's due to visit there, I told him I wouldn't need to go, too. But we will now—and we'll arrive just after he does. We shall see what we shall see!"

Curie's mind was racing. How did the Unsinkable Molly Brown fare and will Artemis' own team try to sink her ship?

That afternoon, the kids and their father thanked Ida Mae for her hospitality and hurried south to Mrs. Beckwith's house. They heard on the radio that *Hurricane Marie* had indeed changed course just before hitting land, sparing the coastline a direct, devastating hit. Their trip south was painfully slow as the rickety van navigated around closed roads, downed power lines, and never-ending debris.

"Dad, look at that trailer park! Those poor people!" Curie cried, as she watched families digging out personal belongings from mobile homes tipped over, ripped apart, or partly crushed by massive tree limbs. Many houses had been moved off their foundations or lost large sections of their roofs.

"Look!" Nick yelled, as he pointed to the left. "That steer is swimming!" Curie and Artemis burst out laughing. A twelve-foot-high fiberglass statue of a bull, probably blown from the steak house lawn across the street, had landed feet first in somebody's swimming pool.

The Masters listened to the radio for more reports of the aftermath of the storm. Storm surges had caused some coastal flooding. Low-lying areas were hit hardest.

"I hope Mrs. Beckwith lives on high ground," Curie said.

"She does," Artemis answered. "I asked her. It's some of the highest land in the area. I just hope she isn't surrounded by water and we can't get to her!"

As they reached Biloxi and moved off the main highway, it was hard to find the local streets because so many street signs were down, twisted, or blown away. The GPS device helped Artemis know where to make a turn. However, deep puddles or actual flooding in some spots caused time-consuming detours. They slowly rolled into the older neighborhood where Mrs. Beckwith lived. Artemis took a turn and stopped the car abruptly in the street. "There's her house!" he shouted, deeply relieved. "It looks pretty good for a hurricane just blowing through last night!"

CHAPTER SIXTEEN:

LOOT TO BOOT

Curie had her eye elsewhere—on a van parked in front with the words *Build 'Em Strong* on the side. "That looks like the van we saw!" she cried. "Is that Oscar's van?"

"Yes, it is," Artemis replied.

"Let's park behind the bushes here so they can't see us," Curie suggested.

"I hope you are wrong about what they are doing!" Artemis said, scowling.

"I hope so, too!" Curie replied. But as soon as the words left her lips, the Masters gasped as they saw Oscar and Red removing a wide-screen television from Mrs. Beckwith's house.

"Curie, take a picture of that with your cell phone camera!" Artemis ordered as he dialed 911, praying there would not be a busy signal. When the 911 operator came on the line, Artemis explained the problem. Fortunately, a police car was just around the corner.

Artemis quickly explained the situation. "Here, I have pictures," said Curie, showing off her cell phone snapshots. "Good job, young lady!" the policeman said.

Suddenly, another police car arrived. The cars surrounded Oscar's van.

"Halt right there!" ordered one of the policemen, as Oscar and Red appeared at the doorway with a computer and DVD player. "You're under arrest for looting!"

One of the officers handcuffed Oscar and Red and shoved them into a police car. They glared at Curie and Nick as the car sped down the street. "Good riddance," Nick mumbled.

But where was poor Mrs. Beckwith while all this was going on?

CHAPTER SEVENTEEN:

COME OUT, COME OUT, WHEREVER YOU ARE!

Along with the other policeman, the kids entered the house to search for Mrs. Beckwith. Artemis inspected the outside of the house to check for damage and the effectiveness of his ties and bindings. He was thrilled! The house had suffered some wind damage, but its roof was secure and it was steady on its foundation.

The kids were not so lucky in their search. They couldn't find Mrs. Beckwith in the usual first-floor rooms. They tried the kitchen.

"I thought Dad said she had a hurricane survival kit," Curie said, as she looked in the cupboard. "There's only the usual amount of food in here, not bottled water, canned goods, first aid stuff and all the rest! Most people would store that here or in the basement."

"The house only has a wine cellar," Nick said. "I already looked."

"I don't even hear Dixie barking," Curie remarked warily. "Remember how Dixie yapped when strangers came to the door?"

Nick agreed. "That dog could make more noise than a hurricane, or you, Curie, when you get in a fit!"

"Look who's talking!" Curie retorted.

The policeman and the kids climbed the stairs to the second floor. All the rooms were neat and clean, but empty of Mrs. Beckwith and her dog. Again, there were no supplies for a hurricane.

"Wait!" Curie said excitedly, "I remember Mrs. Beckwith saying that a

well-built attic was the safest place to be during a storm with flooding—just like Ida Mae's idea. I wonder if she's up there!"

"How do we get up there?" the policeman asked.

"Through a hallway in the back," Artemis said, as he noisily stomped upstairs from his outdoor house inspection. "Follow me," he said. But when they got to the end of the hall, they couldn't find the steps to the attic.

"I know we came this way," Nick stated firmly. "I distinctly remember seeing steps beyond this window on the left. There's a bookcase here now."

"The passage to the attic must be a secret passage!" Curie cried, ever the sleuth. "I'll bet there's a secret latch in the bookcase that will turn to the right, and let us in!"

"You're right," Artemis said, proud of his daughter's analytical abilities. "I remember this bookcase was set against the right wall!"

Curie pushed a few books aside and felt for anything unusual along the right side of the bookshelf. In a moment, her deft fingers found a spot that gave way to pressure. She pushed.

"Abracadabra!" Curie recited, as the bookshelf slid slowly back and to the right, becoming flush against the right wall. In front of them were the steps to the attic. Curie and Nick bounded up the steps, followed by Artemis and the policeman. Artemis suddenly sneezed. ᴀᴄʜᴏᴏ! ᴀᴄʜᴏᴏ!

"Dixie must be somewhere near," Nick said. "Dad's allergies are acting up!"

At the top of the stairs, the group met another closed door. It was locked. As they banged on the door, they heard the raucous yapping of what could only be Dixie!

When Mrs. Beckwith opened the door, Curie fell into her arms and gave her a big hug. "Thank goodness we found you!" she cried.

"You must have known I would survive, didn't you?" Mrs. Beckwith said with a sparkle in her eye. "Look around me."

Everyone was stunned to find a complete emergency storage unit that could have kept 10 people alive for 20 days. Shelves of bottled water, canned goods, and all sorts of disaster preparedness kits lined the walls.

"This room used to be a safe haven for slaves trying to escape north to the Underground Railroad," Mrs. Beckwith said with pride. "It has a long history of protecting people. This time, it has protected Dixie and me very well."

"That's why there was a secret passage!" Curie cried, now understanding the strange entrance to the attic.

"You guessed it," Mrs. Beckwith said. "Well, I suppose it's safe to go downstairs. How about some lemonade?"

CHAPTER EIGHTEEN:

AN ATTITUDE OF GRATITUDE

In the kitchen, the policeman explained about the two men arrested for looting Mrs. Beckwith's house. He added that, thanks to the Masters' help, the stolen goods were still on the property, out front in the team's van.

Artemis apologized for his team's behavior, and between bouts of sneezing, told the old lady that his two kids became suspicious early on. He told her the whole story—Curie's concern about the blogs, the warnings, and the stolen laptop.

"I have you, Artemis, to thank for making my home so secure," Mrs. Beckwith said warmly, "and I have two wonderful children to thank for looking after me and my things. I didn't even know those two men were downstairs. And neither did Dixie. She didn't bark at them—but then, she's not well. I'll take her to the back room so you can stop sneezing, Artemis!" Mrs. Beckwith stroked her dog's head as she carried it down the hall.

"Nick and I will get Mrs. Beckwith's TV and DVD," Curie said to Artemis.

As Nick climbed into the back of the team's van to get the stolen DVD player, he saw something familiar.

"Curie," he yelled. "Guess what? Here's my laptop!"

"Yesssss!" Curie cried. "Now I can get mine back full time!"

When all the work was done, it was time to say goodbye. Mrs. Beckwith walked the Masters family out to their van. "My, look how

tranquil the sky is!" she remarked. "By looking at it, you would never believe we were hit by such a powerful storm!"

"Dad, are we still going to Florida?" Nick asked hopefully. "I heard there's another tropical depression heading there!"

Artemis laughed. "Haven't you had enough of hurricanes?" he teased. "Wait until you see the mountains of reports you and Curie need to type up!"

Curie and Nick groaned.

Mrs. Beckwith laughed. "I can see they're like me," she said, "they thrive on the excitement but you have to prod them to do the grunt work! Artemis, they are unsinkable!"

Curie and Nick beamed at the praise from this great lady. Both kids wrapped themselves around her in a Category 5 hug!

THE END

ABOUT THE AUTHOR

 Carole Marsh is an author and publisher who has written many works of fiction and non-fiction for young readers. She travels throughout the United States and around the world to research her books. In 1979, Carole Marsh was named Communicator of the Year for her corporate communications work with major national and international corporations.

Marsh is the founder and CEO of Gallopade International, established in 1979. Today, Gallopade International is widely recognized as a leading source of educational materials for every state and many countries. Marsh and Gallopade were recipients of the 2004 Teachers' Choice Award. Marsh has written more than 50 Carole Marsh Mysteries™. In 2007, she was named Georgia Author of the Year. Years ago, her children, Michele and Michael, were the original characters in her mystery books. Today, they continue the Carole Marsh Books tradition by working at Gallopade. By adding grandchildren Grant and Christina as new mystery characters, she has continued the tradition for a third generation.

Ms. Marsh welcomes correspondence from her readers. You can e-mail her at fanclub@gallopade.com, visit carolemarshmysteries.com, or write to her in care of Gallopade International, P.O. Box 2779, Peachtree City, Georgia, 30269 USA.

BOOK CLUB
TALK ABOUT IT!

1. Who was your favorite character? Why?

2. What was your favorite part of the book? Why?

3. Do you think Mrs. Beckwith should have stayed at her house through the storm? What would you do if a bad storm was on its way to your house?

4. Have you ever been in a hurricane or a bad storm? Discuss how you felt and describe what the storm was like.

5. Some of the people who lost their homes in *Hurricane Katrina* had to live in FEMA trailers and didn't have much privacy. Discuss how you would feel if you had to live in a FEMA trailer for a month.

6. David Logan explains to Nick and Curie that it's not looting if you take things that you need to survive, but it is wrong to steal things like TVs or DVD players. Discuss the difference between necessity and greed. Do you think David Logan should pay back the grocery store for the food he needed?

7. When Nick and Curie realize that something bad is going to happen to Mrs. Beckwith, they tell their father. What would you do if you thought someone was in danger? Who would you go to for advice? Do you think Nick and Curie did the right thing?

BOOK CLUB
BRING IT TO LIFE!

1. Let's blog! First, create your own user name (like RedRooster). Be creative! Then, have each member write his or her user name and a question at the top of a piece of notebook paper. Pass your "blogs" around the group. Answer the question the person asked, and create a new question for the next person. Keep passing until your piece of paper has made it all the way around the group. Then read your silly conversations out loud.

2. Be prepared! Imagine a storm is coming and your book club is stuck in the house! Have each member find an item for a hurricane survival kit. Be sure to collect bottled water, canned food, a can opener, a flashlight, and some batteries. You might even want to include some games to pass the time. Be creative!

3. Map your own evacuation route! Find a map of your state. Decide as a group what would be the best way to escape if a hurricane was on the way. Trace the highways with a highlighter so you won't forget the way!

4. Let's get naming! Ask each member of the group to make up as many hurricane names as they can, using the first letter of their first name. The one with the most hurricane names wins!

GLOSSARY

askew: turned or twisted to one side

defer: to delay for a later time

forsake: to abandon or leave someone who needs you

immerse: to plunge or throw into completely

levee: an embankment that is built to keep a river from overflowing

sedentary: an activity that requires little activity, like sitting

sleuth: another name for a detective

subside: to wear off or die down

tranquil: calm, not agitated

HURRICANE TRIVIA

1. A hurricane is most destructive during its first 12 hours onshore.

2. The hurricane is the world's biggest storm.

3. *Hurricane Katrina* cost $75 billion in damages— the most expensive hurricane in U.S. history.

4. Ten minutes of one hurricane has as much energy as a nuclear bomb. That's one strong storm!

5. Every hurricane has an "eye" where the wind is perfectly calm and the sky can even be sunny!

7. If a hurricane is really big and destructive, its name is retired and never used again for any other hurricane.

8. A group of pilots called the Hurricane Hunters actually fly right into the eye of a hurricane so they can track how the storm is developing! Pilots say that it feels like "you're on a roller coaster going down, and then getting shot back up again," while they are in the eye wall.

9. Hurricanes always form and gain power over the water, but they die quickly when they reach land.